Ollie's First Year

text by Jonathan London

illustrations by Jon Van Zyle

University of Alaska Press

Fairbanks

Springtime in the northern mountains.

In an otter's den (once a beaver lodge),
    the nest of moss and grass
is fluffed and ready.

    It is time!

First one pup is born . . .
    and another . . .
then Ollie slithers out—
the third, and smallest, of the litter.

Blind and toothless,
he nuzzles with his brother and sister
    and suckles Mama Otter's
warm, rich milk.
    Slurp slurp slurp!

For five weeks, Ollie and his siblings
    suckle and grow
in the darkness of the den…
    then their eyes open
for the very first time!

Finally, in the middle of summer,
Ollie and the other kits
leave the den for the first time—
        to romp ...
and chase ...
        and wrestle
on the banks of the rushing river.

(Ollie is tough for such a little guy!)

Weeks later, when their fur has fully grown in
like waterproof coats,
it's time for swimming lessons!

Mama Otter carries the kits
by the scruff of their necks
to the river's edge,
then one by one,
she drops them in . . .

plop! plop! plop!

Ollie squeals and splashes—
   splash! splash! splash!
Then Mama Otter shows the pups
   how to paddle with their hind feet
and use their powerful tails as rudders.

In a few days, they are
          twisting
     rolling
             darting dancers
   in a graceful underwater ballet.

When Ollie climbs out to play,
      he's the first to scuttle up a mudslide…
and slide back down—

SWOOOOOOOSH!

Splash!

At summer's end, after five months away,
Ollie's father returns
and helps teach the pups

how to corner small fish
against the riverbank . . .

and to root in the river-bottom mud
for crayfish, mud minnows,
and frogs.

By autumn, Ollie
     is nearly full grown.
But he still wants to play!
     Look! He juggles a fallen leaf
     in a cold October pool.

As the days grow shorter and colder,
   his fur grows thicker.
Even in January
   he stays warm with his family
      on the coldest day of winter.

It's time to play again!

Ollie and his siblings take turns belly-sliding down a snow slope—

swOOOOOOOOSH!

But where is Ollie?

He is missing!

He has broken through the ice,
and the rapids have snatched him
away!

He tumbles among boulders
and kicks to the surface for air.
His frantic calls pierce
the wild rush of the river.
Help! Help!

Downstream
through the swirling rapids he goes . . .

till at last he snags a root
    and pulls himself up . . .

and out of the icy water!

But Ollie is all alone!

He shakes water off like a dog—
    whoosh whoosh whoosh!—
and rolls in the powdery snow
so his fur won't freeze.

The sun has gone down
    and the full moon is rising.
Ollie humps and jumps along,
    then slides across the snow—
    hump-jump . . .
then glides through the moonlight.

But he hears a sound! Is it danger?

He stops. His fur bristles.
He twitches his whiskers—
        sniff-sniff-sniff!
What is it?

IT'S HIS FAMILY!

Ollie cries out!
Then they all chuckle
    and tumble and play!

Tired now, Ollie and his family
    slip off the bank
 into a quiet pool—
    slooooosh—
and slide under the ice . . .

        then up into their warm dry den,
where they sleep curled in a mass
of breathing fur.

All winter, when not playing or asleep,
    they swim under ice
chasing fish.
        Swish!

When warmth returns in the spring,
and the ice and snow melt,

Ollie is no longer so little.

He is one year old.

When he is two
he will start a family
of his own.

AUTHOR'S NOTE

There are thirteen species of otter in the world. The otters of this story are North American river otters. They are members of the weasel family, which includes weasels, skunks, muskrats, martins, fishers, badgers, and wolverines. Inhabiting most wilderness areas of North America, they are rare or absent in the dry Southwest, as well as Indiana, Nebraska, South Dakota, and Ohio. They are quite common in the colder climates of North America, especially Alaska and Canada (their Latin name, *Lontra Canadensis*, means "Otter of Canada").

All otters are semiaquatic mammals and spend most of their time in the water. River otters have streamlined bodies, powerful tails, and webbed feet—all good for swimming. They paddle their feet and use their tails, which are one third their entire length, as rudders. If they want to swim really fast, they hold their legs back and flex their bodies, swishing their tails up and down through the water. River otters can swim almost seven miles per hour and hold their breath underwater for up to eight minutes. Flaps in their nostrils and ears close when they dive underwater.

River otters mature and mate at around two years old and usually have a litter of one to six pups in April or May. The mothers use abandoned beaver lodges or other abandoned dens along waterways, which they clean and widen before giving birth. The fathers are often chased away at this point, but many return later and help train the pups how to fish and hunt.

Their main source of food is fish, but they also eat crayfish, frogs, turtles, snails, salamanders and snakes. They'll sometimes even eat berries.

River otters can stay warm in the cold winter. They have a soft, lower layer of dense fur to keep them warm and a long, outer layer of guard hairs, which have a special oil that keeps their underfur and skin dry. Otters do not hibernate during the winter. They sleep in their warm dens, then swim under the ice, if necessary, and dive for fish.

The secretive otter is rarely seen. They're most active at night and stay out of sight. They're best known for their playfulness—a behavior that helps them learn how to survive in the wild.

River otters have been trapped for their fur and at times have come close to extinction. Their predators include wolves, foxes, and mountain lions. But human pollution and loss of habitat is now the biggest problem they face. Thanks to reintroduction and other conservation programs, populations have grown or become re-established in many areas of their natural habitat.

If you ever get the chance to see a frolicking otter at play, you'll hope for their continued survival and may even try to do something about it.

For Michael, Claire & Leah. (JL)

For all the other children. (JVZ)

Published by the University of Alaska Press
P.O. Box 756240
Fairbanks, AK 99775-6240

Library of Congress Cataloging-in-Publication Data

London, Jonathan, 1947–
 Ollie's first year : a year in the life of a river otter / text by Jonathan London ; illustrations by Jon Van Zyle.
    pages cm
 Summary: A playful, young otter learns how to paddle with his hind feet, use his powerful tail as a rudder, and root in the river bottom mud for crayfish.
 ISBN 978-1-60223-228-0 (hardcover : alk. paper) — ISBN 978-1-60223-229-7 (pbk. : alk. paper)
 1. North American river otter—Juvenile fiction. [1. Otters—Fiction.] I. Van Zyle, Jon, illustrator. II. Title.
 PZ10.3.L853401 2014
 [E]—dc23
                    2013024448

This publication was printed on acid-free paper that meets the minimum requirements for ANSI / NISO Z39.48–1992 (R2002)
        (Permanence of Paper for Printed Library Materials).

Printed in Korea